S0-CXV-795

Behind Every Step

Have You Got What It Takes to Be a Choreographer?

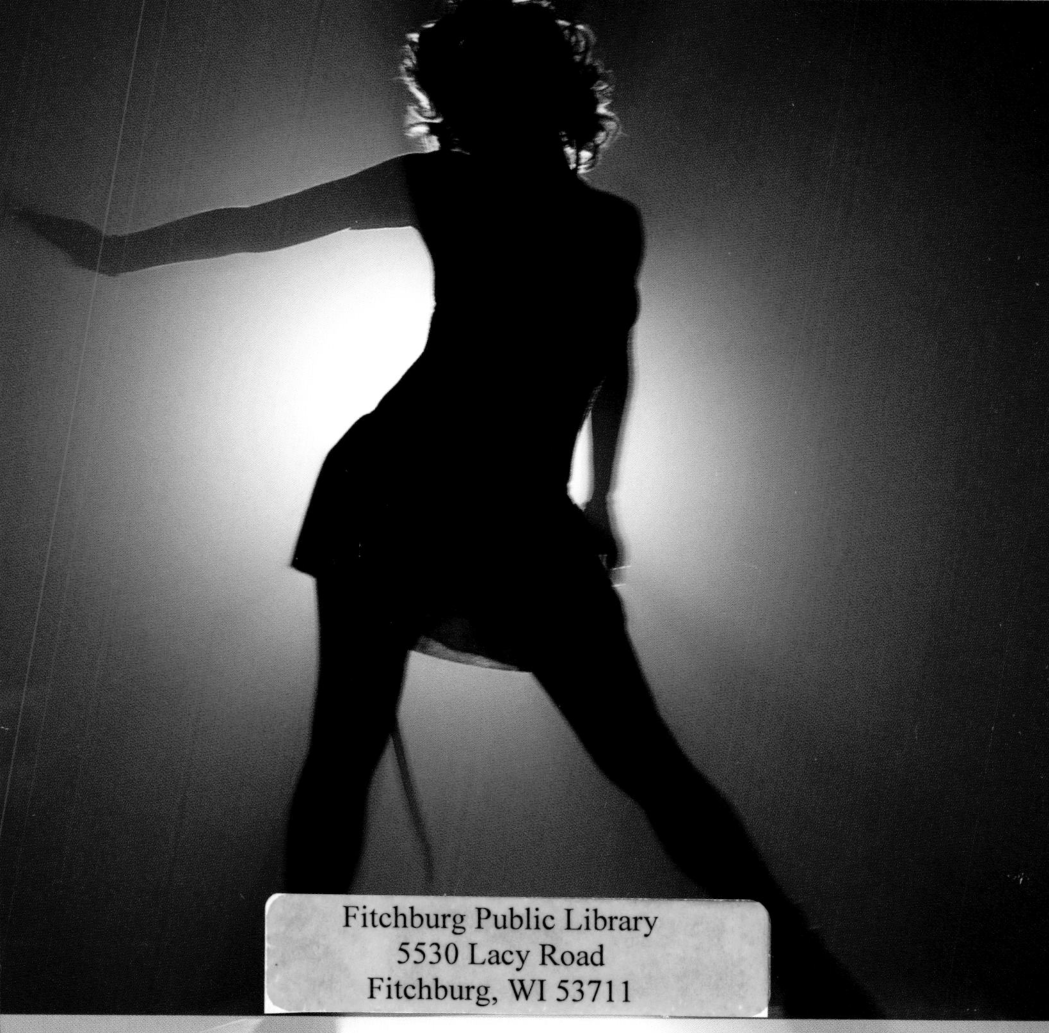

by Lisa Thompson

Compass Point Books Minneapolis, Minnesota

First American edition published in 2009 by
Compass Point Books
151 Good Counsel Drive
P.O. Box 669
Mankato, MN 56002-0669

Editor: Marissa Bolte
Designer: Ashlee Suker
Media Researcher: Wanda Winch
Art Director: LuAnn Ascheman-Adams
Creative Director: Joe Ewest
Editorial Director: Nick Healy
Managing Editor: Catherine Neitge
Content Adviser: Kaita Lepore, Co-Rehearsal Director and Dancer,
SonneBlauma Danscz Company,
Santa Barbara, California

Editor's note: To best explain careers to readers, the author has created composite characters based on extensive interviews and research.

Printed in the United States of America.

This book was manufactured with paper containing at least 10 percent post-consumer waste.

Library of Congress Cataloging-in-Publication Data
Thompson, Lisa, 1969–
Behind every step : have you got what it takes to be a choreographer?/
by Lisa Thompson. — 1st American ed.
p. cm. — (On the job)
Includes index.
ISBN 978-0-7565-4207-8 (library binding)
1. Choreography—Juvenile literature. 2. Choreographers—Juvenile literature. I. Title. II. Series.
GV1782.5.T46 2010
792.8'2—dc22 2009009875

Image Credits: AAP Image/Tracey Nearmy, 17 (b); AFP Photo/DDP/Clemens Bilan, 16 (t); Ho/Paul Kolnik, 17 (t); AP Images, 16 (b); BigStockPhoto.com/afhunta, 38; andyrossy, 43 (t); barsik, 11 (t); Belinda_bw, 19 (t); Gino Santa Maria, 42-43 (back) ; nruboc, 18-19 (back); Paha_L, 7 (t); rban, 6 (m); Yuri_Arcurs, 40 (b); Dreamstime.com/Abrangstudio, 14 (back); Agno_agnus 34 (m); Ajn, 15 (mr); Aleynikov, 12 (t); Carlodapino, 4 (b); Carrydream, cover (front), 8 (b), 30 (t); Claudiodivisio, 31 (b); Darrenbaker, 8 (t); Dleonis, 44 (b); Farek, 11 (b); Fjord, 15 (ml); Forgiss, 3 (bl, br), 7 (b); Friday, 7 (m); Ginaellen, 6 (b); Goodlux, cover (back), 5 (t), 20 (m), 39 (all); Imagecom, 29 (t); Jacetan, 44-45 (back); Jeancliclac, 34 (b); Kovalvs, 45 (t); Logoboom, 14 (b); Madartists, 22-23 (back); Maunger, 40-41 (back), 46 (tl); Miflippo, 27 (t); Nithor, 3 (tl); Novikov, 6 (tl); Off, 10-11 (back); Photoclicks, 28; Rtimages, 32, 33(clipboard); S-dmit, 26-27 (back); Silvanoaudisio, 3 (bm); Spepple22, 33 (b); Talomor, 12 (b); Venakr, 16-17 (back); Yurok, 8-9 (back); Fotolia/James Steidl, 24-25; TEA, 1; Photos.com, © [2009] Jupiterimages Corporation, 10 (all); iStockphoto/anouchka, 35 (m); archives, 4-5 (back); AYakovlev, 30 (m), 37 (b); baytchev, 48 (b); best-photo, 13 (t); DrGrounds, 20 (t); dune915, 18; elkor, 23 (b), 43 (m,b); ericmichaud, 9 (t); FDS111, 29 (b); filo, 6-7 (back), 32-33 (back); Forgiss, 5 (m); Gizmo, 3 (tmr); HelenKoshkina, 46 (b); izusek, 48 (t); JBryson, 33 (m); jodiecoston, 47 (m); joebrandt, 42 (t); jondpatton, 22 (b); joshblake, 3 (tml), 9 (b), 22 (t); kaceyb, 41 (t); kkong5, 11 (m); Kursad, 36 (b); leezsnow, 35 (t); ManoAfrica, 13 (b); Marzdin, 3 (tr); mcpix, 23 (t), 45 (b); Miquelmunill, 36-37 (back); PeskyMonkey, 21 (t); Pobytov, 37 (t,m); Quintanilla, 5 (b); ranplett, 45 (m); RapidEye, 44 (t); redsmiler, 23 (m); Sayarikuna, 14 (m); Soubrette, 34 (t); Stalman, 21 (b); Stockstyle, 20 (b); Timsulov, 41 (b); track5, 41 (m); travelpixpro, 40 (m); webphotographeer, 26 (all), 27 (b), 47 (t); The Benesh Institute, Royal Academy of Dance, London, 31 (t,m); Wikimedia Commons, 35 (b)
All other images are from one of the following royalty-free sources: Big Stock Photo, Dreamstime.com, iStockphoto, Photo Objects, Photos.com, and Shutterstock. Every effort has been made to contact copyright holders of any material reproduced in this book. Any omission will be rectified in subsequent printings if notice is given to the publishers.

Visit Compass Point Books on the Internet at *www.compasspointbooks.com*
or e-mail your request to *custserv@compasspointbooks.com*

Table of Contents

Time to Move!

It is 8 A.M. when I arrive at my dance studio. I don't have classes to teach until after lunch, so I have been using my mornings to choreograph. My dance group, Rise, is performing three dances for the upcoming annual Festival of the Sea.

For the dances, I hired three young local musicians to reflect the festival's theme, "A Day at the Beach." I have been playing the pieces over and over since I received them two weeks ago. I have worked out nearly all the dance phrases and sequences. I play the music again as I stretch and prepare to dance.

Warming up is essential for dancing.

I begin to dance to the music, trying out the steps and movements I have imagined. Some of them work—and some don't. I continue to dance all morning, improvising, taking notes, listening, and letting my body move and create. I jump, step, and repeat movements, and slowly the dances come together. I'm excited—the movements and the music are blending better than I could have hoped. I can't wait to show my dancers the moves this afternoon so we can begin rehearsing. With the festival only six weeks away, there is so much to prepare behind the scenes, too—staging, costumes, lighting, and props. It's going to be a very busy time.

Dance through time

Dance has existed since prehistoric times. Both 9,000-year-old rock shelter paintings in India and Egyptian tomb paintings from around 3300 B.C. depict figures dancing.

How I Became a Choreographer

I was just like these young dancers.

I have always loved to dance and perform. When I was 4 years old, I started ballet and jazz lessons at a local dance school.

I always enjoyed performing in the recitals at the end of the year. I was excited at the thought of being on stage in front of my family and friends. I can still remember the thrill I got from showing them the dances I had learned.

In high school, I continued to take dance classes in the evenings and on weekends. I would make up dances with my friends for fun. That's when I knew that choreography was the job for me. I also began performing at festivals and dance competitions.

I made some great friends at college and on tour.

I went on to study dance and human movement at a performing arts college. After I graduated, I had a successful audition with a small dance company called Wicked Moves. It was a contemporary dance company that toured around the country.

After five years of touring, I formed my own contemporary dance school, and now I choreograph and teach. While I do miss the buzz of performing, I still spend most of my time dancing.

Being able to artistically realize a dance and see it performed is fantastic. Creating dances can be a lot of work, but it is very rewarding and it's what I love to do. There really is nothing else like choreographing—for me it's the ultimate in creativity and freedom.

Dancing in Paris

The first dance school was established by King Louis XIV of France in 1661. The Académie Royale de Danse's first lessons were given in a room at the Louvre in Paris.

What Does a Choreographer Do?

Just as a writer tells a story or expresses an idea using words, a choreographer translates stories, ideas, and moods into movements and sequences for dancers to perform. The word *choreography* comes from the Greek words *choros*, meaning dance, and *graphia*, meaning to write down.

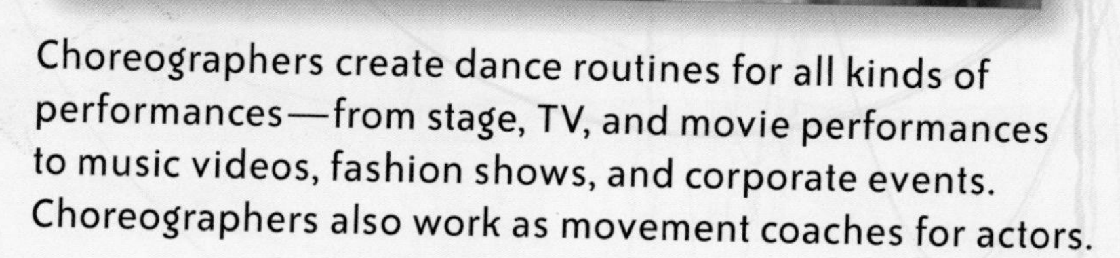

Choreographers create dance routines for all kinds of performances—from stage, TV, and movie performances to music videos, fashion shows, and corporate events. Choreographers also work as movement coaches for actors.

Choreographers need excellent communication skills to explain their ideas. Dancers follow a choreographer's instructions, so they need to understand what the choreographer wants them to do.

Like me, very few people earn enough money from choreography alone. Most choreographers are also teachers, dancers, or company artistic directors.

Teaching can be very rewarding.

Skills needed to be a choreographer:

- passion for dance
- very quick "eye" to analyze moves
- excellent physical fitness
- strong spatial and body awareness
- excellent leadership abilities
- high level of focus
- excellent organizational skills
- ability to handle pressure
- determination to succeed

Tasks can involve:

- developing ideas and turning them into a finished performance
- choosing music
- planning movements to fit music
- auditioning and selecting dancers
- rehearsing and teaching dances
- meeting with producers, costume designers, and musical and artistic directors
- recording the steps on paper or film

Dance Through the Ages

Portrayals of early dance, such as artifacts and cave paintings, show that dance was one of the first arts of ancient society. It existed long before written language. Dance was mainly for ritual purposes, such as praying to the gods, celebrating events or victories, connecting spiritually with ancestors, and telling stories.

Dancers on a fifth century Greek vase

Sioux warriors dancing in the 1800s

Muslim Whirling Dervishes dancing in worship

Ancient dancers

In ancient Greek mythology, Terpsichore was the goddess of dancing.

The Hindu god Shiva was thought to take the form of Nataraja (Lord of the Dance) and perform a dance of creation and destruction.

The Aztecs of Mexico had a god called Xochipilli who was a god of music, love, flowers, and dance.

As human communities became more complex, dancers became highly valued as performers. Those who created dances long ago used the same raw material that choreographers use today—the human body.

modern dance

break dancing

That's a lot of shoes

For some professional ballet dancers, pointe shoes only last a performance or two.

Examples of dance styles

- folk (clogging, maypole dancing)
- ballet
- modern and contemporary
- tap
- jazz
- ballroom (waltz, fox-trot)
- Latin American (mambo, tango, samba)
- street (hip-hop, break dancing)
- swing (rock 'n' roll, jive)

Styles are constantly changing as new dances are created.

ballroom moves

The Body as an Instrument

A choreographer brings a dance to life through the bodies of his or her dancers. Many dances focus on a particular part of the body for expression.

The head and face are most important in Indian Kathakali dancing.

Head

In many Indian and Southeast Asian dances, the head is an important part of the dance. The head, eyes, eyebrows, and mouth are all used to help tell the story of the dance.

Arms

Most dances use the arms. Arm movements can be strong, graceful, percussive, flowing, or vibrating.

Elbows

In many European folk dances, dancers place their hands on their hips so that their elbows point out to the sides. Couples may also link arms and spin each other around.

Hands

Dancers from Southeast Asian cultures spend countless hours learning the dozens of hand shapes and gestures of their dances. Movements vary from being slow and controlled to trembling and frenzied.

Stomach

Skillful belly dancers can make their stomachs shake and ripple. Belly dancing is one of the most commonly improvised dances.

Legs

The legs give the body its movement. Often it is what the legs do that defines the range of movement on stage.

Knees

Many indigenous dances use the half-squat position to emphasize the angles of the knees and to create sharp, percussive movements.

Ballerinas make the most of their legs.

Many African dances use the knees.

Choreograph this!

Although used mainly for dance, choreography is also used in:

- gymnastics
- figure skating
- cheerleading
- marching-band performances
- synchronized swimming
- stage combat (fight choreography)

Feet

Foot stomping is an expressive and defining part of dance—from the elegant glide of a ballet dancer, or the tap of a tap dancer, to the stamp of the flamenco.

The World of Dance

Almost every culture has its own form of dance. Some date back thousands of years, while others have been created more recently to express new ideas. Energetic, soulful, political, educational, or playful, all these dances bring people together.

hula

North America

- Native American dances
- Inuit drum dances
- fox-trot, jazz, rock 'n' roll, disco, hip-hop
- hula (Hawaii)

Caribbean

- limbo (Trinidad)
- mambo (Cuba)
- salsa

morenada

tango

South America

- samba (Brazil)
- morenada (Bolivia)
- tango (Argentina and Uruguay)

hora

Europe

- Highlands dancing (Scotland)
- Morris dancing (England)
- cancan (France)
- flamenco, paso doble (Spain)
- waltz (Austria)
- polka (Czech Republic/ Slovakia)
- ballet (Italy)
- sirtaki (Greece)
- hora (Romania, Israel)

Asia

- belly dancing (Middle East)
- Bollywood-style dancing (India)
- Chukchi traditional dancing (Russia)
- sword and dragon dances (China)
- nihon buyo (Japan)

sword dancing

Masai jumping dance

Africa

- Bushman trance dances (South Africa)
- soukous/African rumba (Congo)
- Masai jumping dance (Kenya/Tanzania)

Australia

- indigenous (Aboriginal)
- bush dancing

Aboriginal dancing

Famous Choreographers

Martha Graham (1894–1991)

Martha Graham was an American dancer who became one of the best-known choreographers of the 1900s. She was a pioneer of contemporary dance. She invented a new dance style that was raw and emotional, rather than the dreamlike, glamorous dancing that was popular at the time. Her technique of contraction and release revolutionized modern dancing and is still used today.

The Martha Graham Dance Company performs

A lifetime of dedication

Martha Graham gave her last performance at the age of 76 and choreographed 181 works over 60 years. In 1998 *Time* magazine called Graham one of the most important people of the century.

George Balanchine (1904–1983)

George Balanchine, who was born in Russia, choreographed his first dance while still a teenager. In 1924 he left Russia to gain more creative freedom. He became a choreographer at the famous Ballets Russes dance company in Paris. In 1933 Balanchine moved to the United States, and in 1948 his dance company officially became the New York City Ballet. He choreographed more than 400 dances and was the head of the company until his death.

Three of Balanchine's early works were performed to mark the 100th anniversary of his birth.

Matthew Bourne (1960–)

Matthew Bourne is a famous British ballet dancer and choreographer. He founded his own dance company in 1987 and created a new version of the famous ballet, *Swan Lake,* in 1995. The traditionally female roles of the swans were all danced by men, which was controversial and exciting. His *Swan Lake* was featured in the closing scene of the film *Billy Elliott*. He continues to create both adaptations and his own original dance pieces, which his dance companies perform around the world.

Matthew Bourne's male version of Swan Lake

Who's Who in a Dance Studio

It takes more than a choreographer to create a dance performance. Here are some of the other people who might be involved.

Artistic director
This person is often also the choreographer. He or she decides what shows to put on and chooses dancers for the roles. The creative vision and direction of every company rests with its artistic director.

Dance teacher
The dance teacher runs daily classes and gives individual coaching to dancers. He or she keeps everyone in shape and ready to go.

Wardrobe supervisor
This job involves taking care of costumes, including renting, cleaning, and repairing costumes.

How many?

Dance companies vary widely in size. Small companies might have just an artistic director/choreographer, administrator, and dancers. They then hire freelance staff members as needed or use the theater staff where they're performing. Large companies could have all these staff members and many more.

Technical director

The technical director coordinates the dancers and stage crew at the performance venue. He or she is responsible for making sure all the technical equipment is clean and safe.

Stage crew

The crew looks after the electronic equipment, such as wiring and special effects. The crew also sets up and operates the scenery, lights, sound, props, and rigging for a production.

Is that light fastened in properly?

Marketing director

A marketing director orders posters and leaflets to advertise shows, and arranges media photo shoots and interviews. He or she also designs and organizes programs to sell at the performances.

General manager

The general manager arranges tour dates, pays salaries, and handles all general business matters. He or she keeps the company running from day to day.

Behind the scenes

It takes many people to stage a dance performance. Many of them you'll never see. Behind-the-scenes people might include:

- lighting riggers and operators
- electricians and carpenters
- designers (costumes, set, sound)
- receptionists/administrators
- physical therapists

The Creative Process

The initial idea for my choreography can come from anywhere—listening to music, watching people on the street, something I've read, or just my desire to express a particular feeling or emotion.

beginning of the process

I may work alone for a long time to build up the dance. Or I might get straight to work with my dancers, allowing them to help me develop my ideas.

There are many ways to choreograph.

While I like to begin my creative process with improvising, there are many ways to approach choreography. It can be a very structured process, with the steps carefully mapped out for the dancers to follow exactly. Or it might be a rough idea that the choreographer works on with the dancers to create the finished dance.

Dance form or martial art?

Capoeira is an African/ Brazilian martial art that blends dance, music, singing, and acrobatics. Modern *capoeiristas* jump, flip, turn, and lunge to try to catch their partners off guard. The focus is on skill, rather than harming one's opponent.

I always tell my dancers to be open to different ways of working. Improvisation is a wonderful way to find fresh ideas. However, knowledge of dance techniques will help the creative process.

Modern feet

As opposed to ballet, which is about resisting gravity, modern dance uses the weight of the body in relation to the ground. Dancing in bare feet enables the dancer to connect directly with the floor. Over time, the soles of a dancer's feet adjust and toughen. Some modern dancers put tape on their toes and the balls of their feet to make it easier to turn and slide.

a modern dancer connecting with the floor

Get the Message Across

To choose the right style for my dance, I need to identify what I am trying to communicate to the audience.

Do I want to tell a story?

Literal (narrative) choreography

Dances that contain a message or communicate a story to the audience are examples of literal choreography. In the early years of modern dance, it was traditional to design dances this way. Dancers used movements instead of words to tell stories. Many famous 19th century ballets, such as *The Nutcracker* or *Giselle*, tell clear stories.

Do I want to represent an essence or feeling?

Choreography using abstraction or patterns

While they don't tell a story, these dances still draw from life and contain the essence of real experience. For example, a dance containing an abstraction about the sea or seashore might contain dance movements that mimic movements of the sea. A dance that is an abstraction suggests the idea of something, not the thing directly. These dances may be used to express feelings, such as revenge, delight, or freedom. They can also be used to create fantasy dances, such as those performed by Cirque du Soleil.

Do I want to explore movement?

Nonliteral choreography

These dances experiment with movement instead of telling a story. While they are dances of mood, they are as structured and choreographed as any narrative dance. Examples include Mikhail Fokine's *Les Sylphides* or Balanchine's *Jewels*.

Nonliteral dances focus on movement.

Setting the Stage

As a choreographer, I must understand how dance movements work on stage. It's not enough to create a beautiful dance in the studio that looks terrible when performed on a real stage. Here are some industry secrets to using a stage.

Center stage is both the strongest and weakest part of the stage. For a climax it can be strong, but spend too much time there and the performance becomes dull and boring.

Upstage corners are good for entrances.

upstage center

upstage right

center stage

Moving forward in a straight line toward the audience is confrontational. That's fine if the choreography intends that, but bad if it's accidental.

downstage right

Corners have a sense of privacy—it's as if the audience is looking in on something.

Stage types

There are three main types of stages:

- proscenium stage—audience sits in rows in front of the stage, with the sides and back hidden from view
- thrust stage—audience sits in rows around three sides of the stage, with the backstage area still private
- arena stage/theater-in-the-round—audience surrounds the stage and can see dancers coming on and off stage

PUN FUN The ballet shoes argued that they had a pointe.

The sides of the stage are very weak. Spending time there is not recommended.

upstage left

The middle of the side is the worst place to enter or exit—or to do anything at all, really.

downstage left

Downstage corners are good for exits.

Shaping the Dance

Choreographers use various musical structures to shape their dances.

AB

The AB form has two parts. Part A presents a series of moves. Part B then presents a contrasting theme. For example, the A form might be large movements and be performed high up, while the B form is slow and closer to the floor. The choreographer must create a smooth transition to move from one part to the other.

This time part A is a little different.

ABA

The ABA is the same as AB, except after B, A is performed again, but with a twist. Again, skillful use of transition between the sections is needed.

Suite

The typical suite has a moderate beginning, a slow second section, and a fast and lively third section.

Variation tricks

A variation can be made by:

- changing the tempo, rhythm, or direction of movements
- changing the structure, style, or mood of the theme
- repeating or lengthening parts of the theme and leaving out other parts
- changing the number and placement of dancers

This would look very different with more dancers.

Rondo

In the rondo, the A phrase is a repeated theme throughout the piece, with many different phrases in between—for example, ABACADA or ABCACBD.

Theme and variations

A theme is presented, then repeated with changes, while still keeping the original theme recognizable. The theme is usually explored in several variations.

The theme can be a single phrase of movements or several movement phrases put together into a sequence.

The timing and movement of the original sequence must remain throughout the dance. Using themes and variations is both challenging and helpful to the choreographer, and it provides a framework for movement choices.

New themes can be introduced for variety.

Choreography Secrets

Choreography theory can be studied at colleges and universities as well as at dance schools. I learned my skills both by studying and by watching choreographers at work. I'm still learning now! There are some key ideas and tips that are valuable to know.

Don't be a slave to the music—be guided by it, but feel free to use contrasting dance movements, too.

Don't have your dancers turn their backs to an audience for too long. It's hard for the audience to stay connected to what's happening on stage if they are looking at people's backs.

Movements that feel fast and strong to a performer can appear slower and weaker to the audience. Check how the movements look, not just how they feel to you.

Circular movements are powerful on stage and should only be used when building up to the climax of a dance.

Knowing when to stop is an important skill. It's easy to keep going when you're excited about the choreography. Beware of creating a dance that is too long—instead, leave the audience wanting more.

The end of a dance carries a lot of weight. It is a large part of what the audience remembers when they leave. Take time to create a strong ending.

Leave a lasting impression

Finally, remember to listen to good advice. If your dancers, or other choreographers, are telling you that something doesn't feel or look quite right, don't be too proud to take another look.

International Dance Day

April 29, the birthday of famous French dancer and ballet master Jean-Georges Noverre, is International Dance Day. It was established in 1982 to raise awareness of the importance of dance and to encourage governments to include dance in their education systems.

Observing the dance

Choreographers must learn to look at the total picture they are attempting to create. It is our job to decide whether a dance is working.

Are the moves dynamic, not static?

Are dancers forming groups when they shouldn't be?

Does each piece of the dance lead smoothly into the next?

Is there a sense of continuity?

Is the dance interesting to watch?

These are just some of the many questions I must ask myself when watching a dance.

The skeleton wanted to dance but had no body to dance with.

Recording the dance

There are several ways to record a dance, but I find a video camera is the simplest and easiest. I then sit and watch the dance over and over. This allows me to look at it with fresh eyes at various times.

Getting it down

Many choreographers use a combination of words, numbers, lines, and stick figures to plan a dance or to remember what they have already worked out. Most big dance companies employ dance notators to take notes while a new dance is choreographed.

There are two main forms of notation used to record a dance—labanotation and Benesh. Labanotation is used for all kinds of movement, while Benesh is mostly used for ballet. Both systems are logical but complicated. Since the 1920s, many famous dances have been written down, preserving them for future generations.

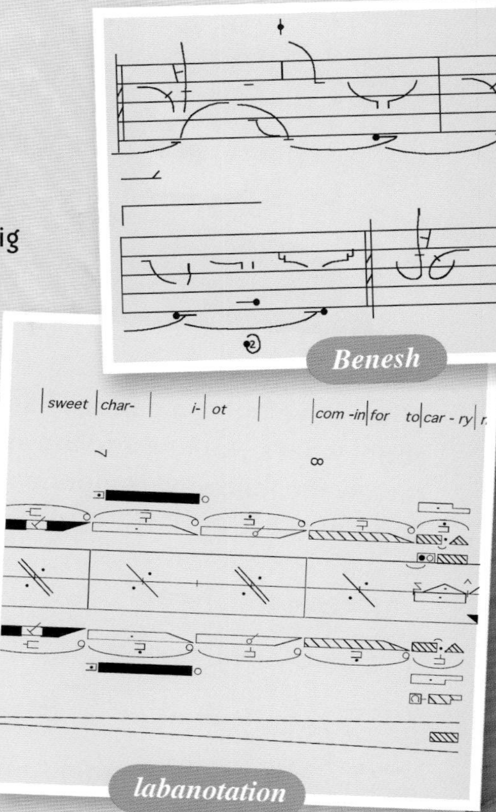

Benesh

labanotation

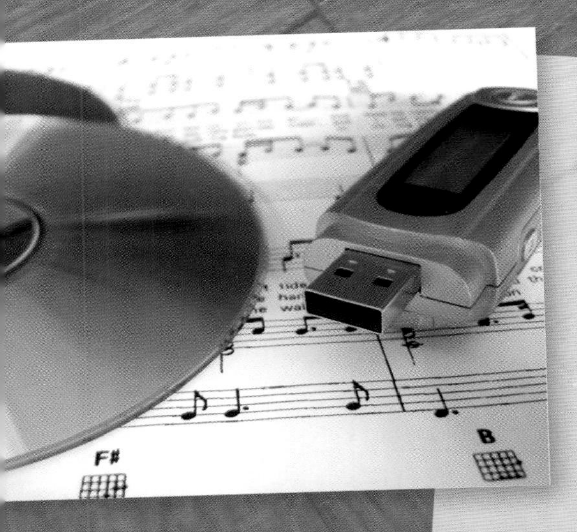

Computers and choreography

Some choreographers use computers to create a dance by manipulating an image of a dancer on screen. They also record a movement and use the computer to build a dance around it. Computers can also store dance recordings.

Assessing the dance

When developing a dance, I like to review it so I have a clear idea about what's working and the areas that need more attention. I review the following components, using 10 as the highest score and 1 as the lowest.

Assessment sheet

- [ ] Overall form of the dance—beginning, middle, end
- [ ] Unity, continuity, flow
- [ ] Variety, movement manipulation, sequence
- [ ] Repetition throughout overall dance
- [ ] Development of dance phrases
- [ ] Relationship between dancers and expression of dance meaning
- [ ] Creative use of body shape
- [ ] Use of stage: awareness of stage space, blocking, stage area, pathways
- [ ] Communication of purpose, feeling, or solution of problem
- [ ] Performance, projection, and overall quality of movement

General comments:

___

___

Planning the performance

Planning a dance performance is a huge task. It helps to break it down into smaller tasks:

- auditions
- rehearsals
  - —blocking rehearsals (working out the positions of dancers)
  - —technical rehearsals (checking how the props and lighting work with the dance)
  - —dress rehearsals (the final run-through in full costume)
- costume design
- stage and lighting design
- prop design
- design of promotional material
- promotion and marketing of the performance material

As a choreographer, I have to manage my time well so the dancers are ready on time. I must be sure to communicate fully with the other departments so they also have enough time to prepare the costumes, lights, programs, and anything else they may need. All these elements come together to make a performance out of a dance.

Conditioning

Dancers and choreographers need to keep their bodies in the best condition possible, both to prevent injury and to dance their best. Dancers' bodies must be strong enough to cope with many hours of practice and performance.

If dancers don't warm up, they are more likely to hurt themselves.

Stretching and conditioning the body in training and rehearsals is often critical to the outcome and success of a performance.

Dancing all night

Dancing is exhausting. Rehearsals require many hours and usually take place daily, including weekends and holidays. If my company is on the road, we usually travel on weekends. Most performances are in the evening, and we rehearse during the day. Dancers must also work late hours. It is important that choreographers understand and promote good body conditioning practices for their dancers.

Pilates

Pilates is a body conditioning method invented by Joseph Pilates in the 1920s. It emphasizes flexibility and coordination and uses breathing techniques to help increase abdominal strength. Many well-known dancers include Pilates in their training because it encourages strength and control without adding bulk.

Royal footwork

Queen Elizabeth I of England (1533–1603) reportedly performed the galliard, a Renaissance dance, for 20 minutes every morning to help keep her body in shape.

Yoga

Yoga is a form of meditation and exercise. Originating in India more than 3,000 years ago, yoga strives to unite the body, mind, and spirit. The physical part of yoga is called hatha yoga. It focuses on shaping the body into certain poses, called asanas, while practicing controlled breathing. Yoga is a great tool for improving flexibility, strength, and balance, and is also used as a relaxation tool for stress relief.

Visualization and Imagery

One way choreographers can convey movement to dancers is through visualization—the ability to see a picture in one's mind and then recreate it in movement.

Today I am beginning a series of visualization exercises with my dancers. I ask them to imagine the water lapping on the shore, turning into wild waves and then into fun, playful surf. We begin to move around the studio as if we were the water, moving like the waves.

I then ask them to move across the studio sideways, with their knees bent, like crabs, or to jump and dive like dolphins.

PUN FUN Dance studios have waltz to waltz carpeting.

We imagine being squawking seagulls, sunbathers on the sand, and surfers on the waves—all the while being aware of the rhythm and beats of the music in the background. It helps get us all in the right frame of mind to communicate the feeling of being at the beach.

Using the space

There are many ways to move:

- forward, backward, sideways
- diagonally, circular
- up, down

forward

Combining directions results in patterns:

- zigzag lines
- right angles
- squares
- arcs

Movement may be presented on different levels:

- on the floor—sitting, kneeling, standing, jumping
- on different planes—horizontal, vertical

Rehearsals

There are practical factors that affect the quality of any performance. Getting enough rehearsal time is fundamental. If the dancers are not ready, the performance will suffer. The dancers must also have the appropriate technical skills to fulfill the demands of the choreography.

For a dancer, practice never ends.

With that in mind, I have worked out a rehearsal plan that I believe will prepare us for the big day without wearing everyone out beforehand. I've carefully considered how to use each dancer's abilities in the best way.

I pin up a schedule for the next six weeks on the studio bulletin board for everyone to see. We will have four rehearsal days a week leading up to the performance. On the weekend and day before the show, there will be full dress rehearsals on the venue stage.

Each of the three dances will have its own group. Two of my most skilled dancers will perform in both the first and the last dances.

After the first two rehearsals, I am able to finalize the positioning of all the dancers.

A group of ballerinas tried on their tutus. Some extra costumes were delivered, but they decided there were tutu many.

OK, now let's rehearse!

Alex, can you extend that leg more as you straighten out?

Now, this is where Sasha splits off as the lonely seagull.

We still need to get that knee bend right. Let's go again, please.

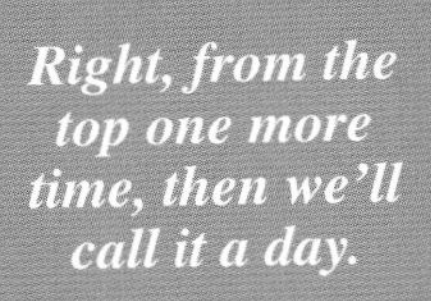

Countdown to the Show

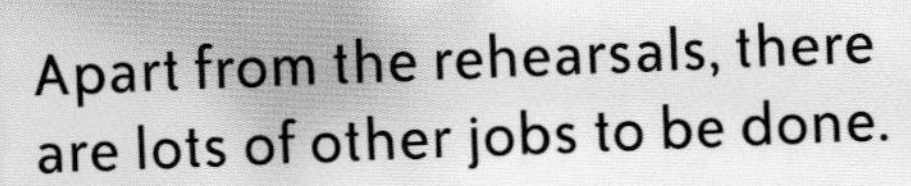

Lots of sewing must be done

Apart from the rehearsals, there are lots of other jobs to be done.

Usually costumes have to be ordered, and each dancer has two costume fittings. For this performance, however, I've chosen very plain dance clothes to give the performance a modern, abstract edge. We'll represent the beach and sea life through our dancing and try to keep the outfits simple.

The lights set the mood.

I meet with the lighting designer to discuss the lighting colors and sequences. He will create the right moods and atmosphere on the stage.

A photographer comes to the studio to snap pictures of some of the dancers, and a journalist will write a feature story for the local paper. Doing this kind of media work is essential to spread the word about the studio and our work. Without an audience, there is no performance.

I give my opinion on the artwork for the posters and flyers announcing the event. I love the shimmering colors the organizers have chosen. They work well with the dance themes I've created. I'm thrilled.

The good news comes a few weeks later—tickets are selling fast!

I meet with the stage manager to go through the program and double-check the stage space for our performance.

Lee, the stage manager

I give makeup instructions to the dancers. For some productions, we have a makeup artist, but for this performance the performers will be responsible for their own makeup.

The dancers and everyone else involved need to have energy and focus to make the performance shine. It's up to me to keep everyone motivated and on track.

Showtime!

1 hour before curtain call
The dancers arrive, change into their costumes, and do warm-up exercises.

35 minutes to go
The dancers touch up their makeup.

15 minutes to go
The stage manager gives the 15-minute warning.

10 minutes before
Individual dance groups assemble at the back of the stage.

5 minutes before
The stage manager calls, "Group one, this is your call!" The first group takes its place in the wings of the stage.

1 minute before
The stage manager cues the lighting operator and the lights dim.

15 seconds before
The lights fade to black ...

PUN FUN He was a tap dancer until he fell in the sink.

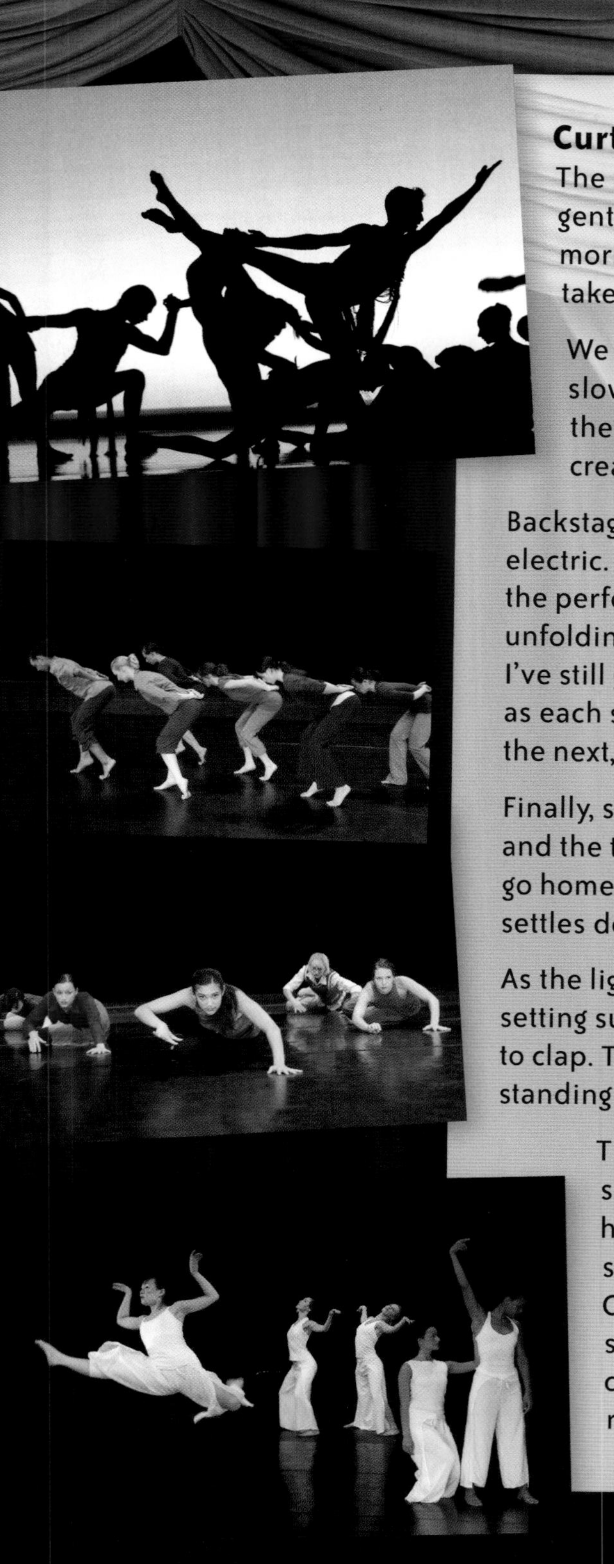

Curtain up!

The music begins as the stage gently lights up in a soft, orange morning glow and the first group takes to the stage.

We start with dawn ... the slow awakening of the beach, the tide coming in, and the creatures stirring.

Backstage the atmosphere is electric. We watch breathlessly as the performers begin to dance. It's unfolding just as I had planned. But I've still got my heart in my mouth as each scene leads effortlessly into the next, showing a day at the beach.

Finally, sunset ... the water cools and the tide goes out, the crowds go home, and the beach's wildlife settles down for the night.

As the lights fade to depict the setting sun, the audience begins to clap. The dancers receive a standing ovation.

The performance is a huge success. All the hard work has been worth it. I am so proud of my dancers. Choreographing a successful show is a wonderful, creative high—I'd recommend it to anyone!

Follow These Steps to Become a Choreographer

Step 1 If possible, study dance, theater, music, and human movement at school.

Step 2 Enroll at a dance school and study as many forms of dance as you can.

Step 3 Get educated. Vocational dance schools offer degrees and diplomas in dance. Some colleges and universities also offer degrees in dance. Coursework may include choreography.

Start young if you can.

Step 4 Join a dance group or form your own. This may provide you with the freedom and flexibility to create and perform your own work.

Step 5 Keep creating! There are many arenas for a choreographer to work in away from the stage, including film, music videos, fashion shows, sporting and corporate events, or as a movement coach for actors and singers.

Red-hot fact

Choreographers need knowledge in many areas of the arts, so it is important to also have an interest in music, art, and design.

Teaching to learn

Many big dance schools give teachers the opportunity to choreograph their pupils' recitals or performances. This is valuable experience that can be gained while earning an income as a teacher or a dancer.

Opportunities for choreographers

In many dance companies, dancers may be asked to contribute to existing choreographic ideas. There are also a variety of other jobs that involve choreography in some way.

Community dance worker—working with community groups to facilitate the expression of the members' ideas in dance

community dance worker

Dance teacher—teaching at dance studios, or owning and running a dancing school (dancers with appropriate qualifications can teach at colleges and universities)

dance teacher

Dance therapist—using dance as part of a therapy program for a wide range of people, including the elderly, or children and adults with special needs or movement disabilities

Find Out More

In the Know

- Most dancers begin formal training between the ages of 5 and 15. Girls usually begin between 5 and 8, while boys start closer to 10 and 12.
- The National Association of Schools of Dance lists 65 accredited university programs in dance throughout the United States.
- There are roughly 26,000 jobs in choreography and dance in the United States, making this field extremely competitive for new job seekers.
- As of 2008, the U.S. Department of Labor estimates that the average hourly wage for a choreographer is $19.04, equaling $39,600 a year. The lowest 10 percent earned $16,620, and the highest 10 percent earned $65,400.

Further Reading

Grau, Andrée. *Dance*. New York: DK Publishing, 2005.

McAlpine, Margaret. *Working in Music and Dance*. Milwaukee: Gareth Stevens Pub., 2006.

Nathan, Amy. *Meet the Dancers*. New York: Henry Holt, 2008.

Internet Sites

FactHound offers a safe, fun way to find Internet sites related to this book. All of the sites on FactHound have been researched by our staff.

Here's all you do:

Visit www.facthound.com

FactHound will fetch the best sites for you!

Glossary

abstract—dance without plot or characters; the dancers' movements and interaction with the audience are used to tell the story

audition—tryout to be a part of a performance

blocking—determining a dancer's movement and position while onstage

choreography—planning and arranging of a theater or dance performance

company—group of dancers dedicated to the creation and performance of dances

conditioning—exercises to reach or maintain physical fitness

contemporary dance—technique and style of dance developed in the 20th century that combines movements and methods from other forms of dance

dance notator—someone who records choreography using a series of symbols and codes

dynamic movement—movement that is capable of change; for example, movement that changes from fast to slow

improvise—using one's environment to create a dance on the spur of the moment

phrase—series of dance movements that have a beginning and end

pointe shoes—also known as toe shoes; type of ballet shoe that allows dancers to perform movements on the tips of their toes for long periods of time

sequence—dance in which a predetermined series of movements is performed

static movement—movement that stays at the same pace

Index

Look for More Books in This Series:

Art in Action: Have You Got What It Takes to Be an Animator?

Battling Blazes: Have You Got What It Takes to Be a Firefighter?

Cover Story: Have You Got What It Takes to Be a Magazine Editor?

Game On: Have You Got What It Takes to Be a Video Game Developer?

Going Live in 3, 2, 1: Have You Got What It Takes to Be a TV Producer?

Head of the Class: Have You Got What It Takes to Be an Early Childhood Teacher?

Sea Life Scientist: Have You Got What It Takes to Be a Marine Biologist?

Trendsetter: Have You Got What It Takes to Be a Fashion Designer?

Wild About Wildlife: Have You Got What It Takes to Be a Zookeeper?